You Are
LOVED

CHARLOTTE GROSSETÊTE

MAURÈEN POIGNONEC

You Are
LOVED

MAGNIFICAT · Ignatius

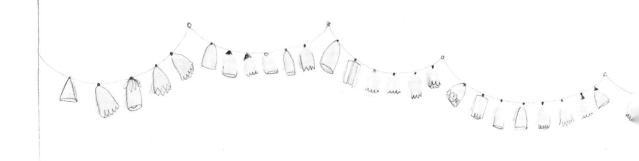

Little one,
we eagerly awaited you
as you grew in Mommy's tummy.
Even before we knew what you looked like,
we already loved you very, very much!

What joy when you were born
and we heard your first cry.
Your head was so tiny
we could hold it in our hands.
What a wonderful gift you are!

Over and over, we rocked you in our arms.
We gave you your name, one we chose just for you.
Your name fits you perfectly,
as though it were made just for you.
Your name is as special as you are.

Time went by.
You began crawling on all fours.
Then you stood up and took your first steps.
Now you can run, and jump, and speak, and sing.
And you eat (almost) everything!
What a joy it is to watch you growing up!

11

When you laugh, we laugh too.
We so love to see you happy!
When you cry, we're sad and we comfort you.
When you're afraid, night or day, we reassure you.
We're always there to protect you.

You are our little treasure.
You are precious to us,
and we love you beyond measure.
Someone else loves you too.
He is bigger than we are,
and his love for you is greater than our own.
His name is God.

Who is God?
God is the one who created the heavens and
the earth. He made everything that lives.
God created you too.

God is the Father of all mankind.
All the people on earth are his children,
and he loves every single one of us.
Each person is special in his eyes, and so are you.
God has written your name on his heart,
and he never forgets you.

To be even closer to you, God came into the world.
He sent his Son Jesus as a child like you.
Jesus had a mommy named Mary.
And God gave him a father on earth.
His name was Joseph.
Jesus was born in a stable.
Mary and Joseph marveled at their little baby!

Jesus grew up.
He learned to walk, to speak,
to sing, and to eat (almost) everything.
Maybe there were nights when he did not like his dinner,
but Jesus was always thankful for his food.

Just like you, Jesus loved
to be hugged by his mommy and daddy.
He loved to hear the stories they told him,
and to go for walks with them.

Joseph and Mary
taught Jesus many things.
Jesus helped the best he could
with his little hands.

Sometimes Jesus made mistakes,
as all children do. Mistakes help children to learn!
Sometimes Jesus was sick or got hurt.
His parents took care of him,
just as we take care of you.

When Jesus laughed,
his parents laughed with him.
When he cried,
his parents comforted him.
His parents loved him very much.

When you feel the warmth of the sun on your skin,
the caress of a breeze, the freshness of rain;
when you smell the scent of flowers,
and watch birds fly through the air;
when you see a beautiful sunset—remind yourself
that little Jesus saw and felt these things too.

When you play with your friends,
know that long ago,
Jesus had friends to play with too.

So, you see, even though Jesus is God,
you two have a lot in common.
Jesus understands you through and through.
Another name for Jesus is Emmanuel,
which means "God with us."
Through Jesus, God is very, very close to you.

Jesus is your friend,
and you can tell him anything.
He wants to know when you feel
happy, sad, or afraid.
He is glad when you feel proud,
and he understands when you feel ashamed.
Jesus listens to you.
He is always right there, helping you
to become the unique person
God created you to be.

Most of all, Jesus teaches you
that you are loved by God.
And he gives you the love you need
so that you can love him and others.

Love your daddy and your mommy.
Love your brothers and sisters,
your whole family, and your friends.
Love God.

The more you love, the happier you will be,
and the closer you will be to Jesus.
Because Jesus is love.

Under the direction of Romain Lizé, Executive Vice President, MAGNIFICAT
Editor, MAGNIFICAT: Isabelle Galmiche
Editor, Ignatius: Vivian Dudro
Translator: Janet Chevrier
Proofreader: Kathleen Hollenbeck
Assistant to the Editor: Pascale van de Walle
Layout Designers: Armelle Riva, Gauthier Delauné
Production: Thierry Dubus, Sabine Marioni

Original French edition: *Tu es unique au monde*
© 2016 by Mame, Paris.
© 2019 by MAGNIFICAT, New York • Ignatius Press, San Francisco
All rights reserved.
ISBN Ignatius Press 978-1-62164-312-8 • ISBN MAGNIFICAT 978-1-949239-01-0

Printed in Malaysia in July 2019 by Tien Wah Press. Job number MGN 19010
Printed in compliance with the Consumer Protection Safety Act, 2008